STAT

SCHOOLED

by *AMAR'E STOUDEMIRE*
illustrated by TIM JESSELL

SCHOLASTIC INC.

This book is dedicated to every parent that takes the time to read with their children. Love you, Mom.

*   *   *

Special thanks to Michael Northrop

ISBN 978-0-545-60607-3

Cover and interior art by Tim Jessell
Original cover design by Yaffa Jaskoll

12 11 10 9 8   17 18/0

Printed in the U.S.A.   40

First printing, September 2013

CHAPTER 1

I took a deep breath. *You can do this*, I told myself. *You've done it before.* I dribbled the ball twice with my right hand and then crossed it over to my left. I looked over at my defender. Correction: I looked *up* at my defender. He was a year or two older than me, and they called him Oakley. It was a good name for him because he was as tall as a tree.

I was isolated one-on-one at the top of the key. We were in crunch time at a weekend basketball tournament. This was the second day, the championship round. I crossed over again, to the right and back to the left. I scanned the court. My friend Jammer was still double-teamed. He'd been scoring all game. But now that the score was tied up late, the other team was doing everything they could to deny him the ball.

That left it up to me. I waited for some traffic to clear in the lane and then made my move. I gave Oakley a quick shoulder fake and then took off to my left. He bit a little on the fake, giving me just enough space to edge by him. He was right behind me, and their center had good position in front of me. There was just a little daylight between the two and it was closing fast. I lofted up a floater. I was sure it would go right over the guy in front of me.

Buh-WONNK!

It never got the chance. Oakley reached out and swatted the thing out of the air. I didn't think he was that close. I turned around and he wasn't: He just had those long arms.

The ball went right to the other team's point guard. Just like that, I had to scramble to get back on defense. I needed good position and active hands to stop Oakley on the other end. I caught a glimpse of the clock. The other team could hold for the final shot — and the win.

We caught a lucky break. Their point guard was fast. He decided to press the advantage and rocket down the court. He was trying to take it all the way in on the break. The lucky break: Our PG, a kid named Jackson, had wheels, too! He stayed with his guy the whole way and bothered him just enough that the shot clanged off the rim.

Jackson got the rebound and led us back up the court as the seconds wound down. We managed to get the ball to Jammer this time. But they doubled him right away, and he had to give it up. Jammer saw me break free and zipped the ball to me. I was in almost the same position as before. And so was Oakley. As a wise man once said, it was déjà vu all over again.

I decided to give the ball up, too. I didn't want a repeat of last time, especially not on game point. I looked for Jackson, but he was lost in all the bodies and limbs near the hoop. As I waited for him to get clear, I saw a familiar face on the other side of the fence.

He was standing there, watching the action — an older guy but in great shape. It was Omar "Overtime" Tanner. He was a local hoops legend and the man who'd invited me to my first big tournament. I was glad to see him, but right now I had to concentrate on this tourney.

But the D was tight. No one was open. Everyone was shouting: "Over here!" and "Switch!" and "Watch the screen!" And then I heard a big voice, deeper than the rest: "Amar'e!" It was Overtime. I kept my dribble low and risked a quick look over.

He raised his big hand up and swirled his index finger around in a quick circle. *Yeah,* I thought. *That just might work. . . .* I crossed over, gave Oakley a quick shoulder fake, and then took off to my left. They were the same moves as last time, and Oakley didn't bite. He was on me tight. I think I even heard him laugh. I know he thought this drive would end with another swat.

Their center stepped in front of me again. I knew that this time he'd be ready for the floater. I busted out the spin move I'd been working on instead. The toughest part was right at the beginning. I needed to keep my handle and try not to take any extra steps. I didn't lose the ball, and the whistle didn't sound, so I figured my footwork was good.

I spun out into the open court and kept going. Oakley barreled right through the space where I used to be and got tangled up with the center. Another dribble, and I laid it up. The ball went in, the horn went off, and the win was ours.

Jammer was named MVP, but he was telling everyone that I was the real star. I waved him off. I hadn't scored half as many points as him. I'd just gotten some good advice at the right time. I got some high fives as I headed off the court.

"Nice move," I heard. It was that same unmistakable voice.

"Thanks, Overtime!" I said. We shook hands. "How'd you know it would work?"

"Aw, just a hunch," he said. "I've been doing this for a looooonnnnggg time."

"Well, it's a good thing," I said. "Because my defender had some looooonnnnggg arms!"

We both laughed.

"You might be seeing him again," said OT.

"Really?" I said. "Are you scouting for another tournament?"

"Might be," he said. He gave me a wink.

I thanked him again, and then he disappeared into the crowd. I had no idea how a man that big could do that. After all these years, I guess he still had some moves.

"Good game, son," I heard.

"Dad!" I said. "I didn't know you were here. I thought you were working today."

"I knocked off early," he said, giving me a hug. "Your brother here talked me into it. Said I was liable to miss a good game. I told him I couldn't have that."

My older brother, Junior, was standing next to him, grinning. "Great move on that last play, STAT," he said. STAT was like a family nickname. It stood for Standing Tall and Talented.

"Thanks," I said, but I could tell he had something else to say. "But?"

"You know you traveled, right?"

"Oh, man." I said. I reached out to punch his arm. He got down into a goofy boxing stance that had all three of us cracking up. I kind of knew he was right. Everyone knew you could get away with a few extra steps at these streetball tournaments. I tried to deny it, anyway.

"I didn't hear any whistle," I said.

Junior shrugged. "Street rules."

"Heads up, STAT," said my dad. "Looks like someone wants to talk to you."

I turned around and saw a man with a microphone in his hand. I recognized him from the local news. Behind him, another guy had a camera on his shoulder. I reached up and straightened my goggles. Then the sports guy started asking me questions.

"Take your time, Amar'e," said Dad. What he meant was: Think before you speak.

"I hear you were the youngest kid in this tournament," said the man, pushing the microphone toward me. "How old are you?"

I was glad it was a question I'd heard before. Some of my friends would probably see this, so I didn't want to say anything stupid.

"I'm eleven," I said. So far, so good. But it didn't seem like enough, so I added, "But in a few months I'll be almost twelve."

Behind me, I heard Dad groan.

CHAPTER 2

Sunday had been awesome, but Monday wasn't going to have any of that. Mondays and awesome just don't mix, you know? So by the time I got to history, with Ms. Bourne teaching, I was ready for something good. History is my favorite subject and we were doing a pretty cool unit on the ancient Aztecs. Ms. Bourne was listing off all the things they invented: everything from a superadvanced calendar to popcorn. Even hot chocolate.

But before she could finish her list, the loudspeaker came on. It crackled for a second and then the school secretary's voice said, "Amar'e Stoudemire, please report to the principal's office."

I just about fell out of my chair. *What did I do?* I wondered.

All Ms. Bourne said was: "Get your things, Amar'e. You are *excused*."

The rest of the class was like, "Ooooooooh," until she told them to be quiet.

Mike was sitting a row in front of me. As I stood up, he gave me a look, like: *What's up?* I just shrugged. I had no idea. I mouthed, "I didn't do anything!"

That's what everyone says, but I really meant it. Whatever it was, every set of eyes in the room followed me as I made my way to the front.

As I closed the door behind me, I heard Ms. Bourne go right back to talking about those inventions. "The first canoe . . . ," she said, but it felt like I was the one who was up the creek.

The halls were empty as I walked to the principal's office. My footsteps echoed in the quiet hallways. Spooky. When I got there, I went up to the desk. "I'm Amar'e. The, uh, principal wanted to see me?"

The school secretary looked up. "Yes, have a seat," she said.

Her voice wasn't friendly or unfriendly. It was just businesslike. I went over and took a seat as she picked up the phone and whispered something into it. Then I just sat there for a few minutes wondering what I'd done.

"Come with me," the secretary said.

I got up and followed her. I'd never been called to the principal's office before, so I wasn't even sure which door to go into. She opened one for me and nodded.

I swallowed hard and ducked inside.

"Have a seat," I heard.

The voice was familiar, but I knew right away it wasn't the principal's.

It was Coach B, our gym teacher. My eyes had adjusted to the dim light now. I could see him standing there and pointing to a chair. For a second, I wondered what the gym teacher was doing in the principal's office. I had gym next period. Would Principal Dumas be there telling me to play volleyball?

"Yes, please," said another voice. "Have a seat."

It was Principal Dumas. I turned and saw her sitting behind a big desk. Everyone seemed really concerned that I have a seat, so I pulled out the chair and sat down. Coach B sat back down in the chair next to mine.

"Uh, hello?" I said. "You wanted to see me?"

"Yes," said the principal. "Actually, it was Jim's idea."

Jim? I guess that was Coach B. I'd never heard his first name. I turned to hear what he had to say.

"Yes, well, I was watching TV last night," said Coach B.

"Okay," I said. "I did some of that, too." I still had no idea why I was here.

"Specifically, I was watching the local news," he said.

"Ohhhh," I said. He'd seen them interview me after the tournament.

"Yes, it sounds like you had a very successful weekend," said Coach B.

"I did all right," I said with a little shrug. I knew Jammer was the real star.

"And they said you were the youngest player there," said Coach B. "Was that for your team or for both?"

"For both," I said. "For all the teams at the tournament, I heard. It was mostly seventh and eighth graders."

"It's funny you should mention that," said Coach B.

"It is?" I said. It didn't seem that funny to me.

"It's the reason we called you in here," said Principal Dumas.

"Wait, was I not supposed to be there?" I asked. "Is there a school rule or something?"

"No, no, nothing like that," said the principal, giving me a big *you're not in trouble* smile.

"It's just that, as you probably know," Coach B began, "we have a team here."

"Yeah, I know," I said. Our school had a basketball team for the seventh and eighth graders called the Bears. He was in charge of it. That's where the *Coach* in *Coach B* came from. "I was thinking about going out for the team next year, when I'm old enough."

"What if I said you didn't have to wait?"

"Ohhhh," I said again. It was starting to make sense. "You want me to play for the Bears?"

"I was talking to Tina about it, and there's a way to make it happen," he said.

I looked over at Principal Dumas. She did kind of look like a Tina.

"So I could play this year?" I said, turning back to Coach B.

"Yes, if you take a few extra steps," he said.

Take a few extra steps? "That's traveling," I said.

Coach B shot me a look.

"Yes, because you're still in sixth grade, you'd need permission from a parent or guardian," he said.

I nodded. I knew I could talk to Dad about it.

"And then we'd have to arrange a tryout, since you missed the real ones."

I nodded again. I'd been through those before for some of the tournaments.

"So what do you think?" said Coach B.

The Bears were good. They'd come within a game of winning their league last year. I thought about those morning announcements. The Bears were always the first thing the day after a game: "Another mighty effort by the Bears!" I remembered the seventh and eighth graders walking around in their jerseys on game days. Everyone thought they were so cool, and they got to take road trips to play other schools.

But then I thought about being the only sixth grader on the team. I wouldn't know anyone, and my friends wouldn't be there.

"Yeah," I said. "Maybe. I mean, I guess. . . ."

I couldn't think of exactly what to say.

"Could really improve your game," said Coach B. "Teach you how to play team basketball."

I looked at him closely. What did he think I did at tournaments, a bunch of one-on-one?

"Take your time," said Principal Dumas. "Think about it."

She slid a piece of paper across her desk. I reached out and picked it up. At the top, in big block letters, it said *PARENTAL PERMISSION FORM.*

"Yeah, take that home, get it signed, and we'll get the tryout going!" said Coach B.

I folded the paper in half.

"Thanks," I said. The first bell went off, and I pushed my chair back. "I have to get to gym."

Coach B let out a little chuckle. "So do I."

CHAPTER 3

My dad still wasn't home from work by the time I got back from school. The good part about that: I had some time to think. Why would the Coach of a team with seventh and eighth graders want a sixth grader? The Bears were good without me.

The bad part: I'd have to wait to talk to my dad. You couldn't just jump up and start talking at him the minute he walked in the door. Dad ran a lawn-care company and it was hard work — I knew because I helped out on the weekends. When he got home, he usually needed to cool his engines in the easy chair for a while. As soon as the truck pulled into the driveway, I could tell today would be no different. He turned the truck off and just sat behind the wheel for a minute, like he was catching his breath.

I went out and helped him unload his equipment and didn't even mention the permission slip.

"How's the job going?" I asked.

"Pretty good," said Dad. "It's a new place. Lot of work, but I think we got the jump on it."

"Your homework done?" he said.

"Yep," I said, and it was, too. I'd been on that as soon as I got home. It was always the first question he asked. And we were still reading about the Aztecs in history, so it was pretty interesting.

Anyway, we finished unloading the truck and then went in and washed up. Dad hit his easy chair and I hit the couch. Once Junior got home, we had an intense video game throwdown. Dad just sat in his chair and watched it like it was TV — it was that good a game!

Finally, after dinner, I had a chance to talk to Dad. "Something crazy happened in school today," I said, putting the last few dishes in the sink.

Dad looked over at me. "Crazy good or crazy bad?" he said.

"Crazy good, I think. Or, I guess I don't really know yet, but definitely interesting. But it started off with me getting called down to the principal's office!"

Now I had his attention! I gave him a quick recap of what had happened. Then I pulled the permission slip out of my back pocket. It was kind of crumpled up from being in my pocket all day. I spread it out on the table and tried to flatten it back out with my hands.

"So you want me to sign that for you?" he said.

I shrugged. "I guess?"

He'd just pushed his chair back under the kitchen table, but now he pulled it out again and sat down. "Step into my office," he said.

I pulled my chair back out and sat down, too.

"It's a pretty good team, right?" he said.

"Yeah, they win a lot. It seems pretty cool."

Dad nodded. "But?" he said.

"But, I don't know, I guess I'm just not sure. I'd be younger than everyone else and I wouldn't know any of them. It'd be a lot easier if Mike and Deuce were there, too. But that won't happen till next year."

"So you think maybe you should wait?"

"Yeah," I said. That was exactly it. "But I don't want to chicken out, either. I mean, I'm not afraid or any-thing. I just . . ."

"No one's saying you are, STAT."

"I think they might, if I don't do it."

"Well, don't worry about them," said Dad. "You were the youngest player at the tournament this weekend, and look how that turned out. Your school team proba-bly wants some new energy."

"Yeah, but it's different in school. Outside, on the playground, you can play or you can't. In school, it's sixth is sixth, seventh is seventh, and eighth is eighth."

"Yeah, I know," said Dad. "I know how boys get — but a basketball court is a basketball court. That's always been true."

"I guess," I said. "But what if —"

Dad waved me off. "All that other stuff, it's a ques-tion of mind over matter. If you don't mind" — we said the next part together — "they don't matter."

I smiled. It felt good to have someone in my corner like that. I looked down at the crinkled permission slip, and he went on: "This is your call, STAT. The question is: Do you want to join the team? Forget about who's there and who's not and what people might think one way or another. Just you: Do you want to join the Bears or not?"

I leaned back in my chair. I looked at him and he looked at me. And just like that, I knew the answer.

"You know what?" I said. "I do. Yeah, I can be a Bear. I know I can hang with those guys on the court. And even if my friends aren't there, it's still kind of like I'm representing them. Those jerseys say 'Bears,' not 'Eighth Grade.'"

"Well, all right," said Dad. "But . . ."

"But what?"

"But you know you're going to have to put in a lot of hours. There are going to be practices, away games, slow buses, and heavy traffic."

"Yeah, I know," I said. I'd thought about that already.

"And you know you still need to get all your homework done, every day," he said.

"Oh, I knooooow that!" I said.

"And you know it doesn't let you off the hook for all your other responsibilities? Helping out around here, pushing a mower now and then . . ."

"I got that," I said.

He gave me a serious look, just to double-check. I gave him a serious nod back.

"Well, that's it, then," he said, satisfied. "Show 'em why I call you STAT."

Dad had been calling me that for years. Standing Tall and Talented wasn't just a nickname; it was a reminder, too. He expected me to live up to it, and I intended to.

He pulled out a pen, reached over, and signed the form. Just like that, I had a tryout to think about. A big one.

CHAPTER 4

*I*t was Tuesday morning, and I had no idea what to do with my permission slip. I tried to hand it in to Ms. Bourne in homeroom, but she didn't know what to do with it.

Deuce was sitting behind me, and he leaned forward to look. "That the form?" he said.

I nodded.

After my conversation with Dad last night, I called up Deuce and Mike to see what they thought. I should have known my boys would have my back. Mike said he and Deuce were planning to try out next year, any-way, and that I could scout out the team for them.

"Aww, yeah," Deuce said, even more excited than the last time we spoke. He held up a hand and I high-fived him over my shoulder.

"Think I should drop it off at the office?" I asked.

"Why don't you give it to Coach B during gym?"

"It's Tuesday, man. We don't have gym." Deuce was smart, but it sometimes took his brain a few periods to activate in the mornings.

"Oh, yeah," he said. "Well, you should just find him, anyways. If you spend too much time down at the office, people are going to start talking."

"All right," I said. "But you come with me."

We got our chance before lunch. Mike went on ahead to get us our usual table in the cafeteria, and Deuce and I headed for the gym. Coach B's office was right next to it.

When we got there, the door was open but the coach wasn't there. Deuce and I looked around the office. It was kind of a cool place. There were stopwatches and whistles hanging from pegs on the wall, a bookshelf that had only trophies on it, and another one that had actual books.

"Maybe I should just leave it on his desk?" I said, pulling out the form.

"Look at that mess," said Deuce. "He wouldn't find it for like ten years —" But before he finished the sentence, Coach B appeared in the door. He was a big man in a small doorway, so we were trapped inside.

"There you are," he said. "I was looking for you. You have your form?"

"Oh, yeah," I said, handing it over.

I thought he might be mad about how wrinkled it was. But he just took a quick look at the bottom to make sure it was signed, and then tossed it onto his desk. It blended in perfectly with the rest of the rumpled papers.

Deuce gave Coach B a little wave, and Coach B nodded back. They knew each other from gym class. Then the coach turned back to me.

"You ready for the tryout?" he said.

"Yeah, I think so," I said.

"Good, I'll see you here after school," he said.

"Wait, what? Today?" I said. I hadn't expected it to happen right away. He hadn't mentioned anything about it yesterday.

"No time like the present," said Coach B. "You have your stuff?"

"Not really," I said. I looked down at my outfit: long-sleeve shirt, jeans, and some fresh new low-top kicks. They weren't really ball sneakers, and I didn't have the goggles I wore for hoops, either.

"Well, that's no problem," said the coach. "We have plenty of spare gear here." He looked around the little office for a second, then plucked something off a chair. It was a pair of small gray polyester shorts that looked straight out of the Charles Barkley era.

"*Great*," I said.

"Well, I'll see you then," he said. "I'm *sure* the guys will be happy to meet you."

He stepped aside to let Deuce and me out of his office.

"Deuce here's a really good point guard," I said. I was hoping maybe he'd let him try out with me.

Coach gave Deuce a closer look as he walked past. He started at his shoes and worked his way up. He didn't have to go too far: Deuce was pretty short.

"Well, I look forward to seeing him next year," said Coach.

So much for that, I thought as we headed toward the cafeteria. I'd be doing this alone. And I'd be doing it in polyester short-shorts.

CHAPTER 5

"Who are you?" said a tall kid standing just inside the gym door.

"Amar'e," I said.

"What are you doing here?"

"Tryin' out."

He pushed a little hiss of a laugh out through his teeth. "Tryouts are over," he said.

I looked around the gym. There were groups of kids bunched up near the baskets at both ends of the court. I'd seen them all before, but I didn't know any of them. Seventh and eighth graders. The sound of a dozen bouncing basketballs echoed off the walls.

"What's he doing here?" I heard.

I turned and saw a second kid talking to the first one, who hadn't even bothered to tell me his name. "He's here for tryouts — only he's about three weeks late!"

The other kid laughed and looked me over. "Nice shorts," he said. Then they both headed over to the nearest basket, laughing their heads off.

I looked down at the tight gray shorts, then at the colorful, flashy low-tops. It definitely wasn't my style to be this mismatched. Coach had given me the too-small shorts and a too-big blueberry-blue T-shirt and told me to get changed. Then he'd disappeared back into his office.

He finally reappeared at the gym door. The whistle was already in his mouth.

TWEEEEEEEEEEET!

Everyone turned to look. A few of them looked at me and laughed.

"Everyone on that end!" he shouted, pointing to one basket. "We're using the other one for a tryout. Kurt, Gerry, get the cones and head on down to this end."

The first guy from before was one of the two kids who broke off from the group.

"We'll start off with a dribbling drill," said Coach B as we walked toward the end of the gym.

"Okay," I said. That didn't sound so bad.

Kurt and Gerry — I had no idea which one was which — sprinted on ahead of us. They were each carrying a stack of orange rubber cones, like the kind you see after an accident on the highway or when some kid pukes in the hall. I hope that wasn't a bad sign.

They began to set them up under the basket. They positioned the cones along the lanes, like they were lining up to rebound a free throw. Then they added the last few along the top of the key.

"What are those for?" I said.

"You dribble in between them," said Coach B. "I'll call out instructions: crossover and between the legs mostly."

"Okay," I said. I could do those moves.

"And then you just touch the top of each cone with your other hand as you pass it."

"You touch the what with what, now?" I said.

But he didn't answer, just pointed to a few cones and told Kurt/Gerry to "even those out."

"All right," he said, turning back to me. "Line up at the start, there."

I lined up in front of the first cone on the left side.

"Give him the ball, Kurt," said Coach B.

The first kid bounced a ball to me. He bounced it harder than he needed to, but at least I finally knew his name.

"Right hand first," said Coach B. Then he stuck the whistle in his mouth and reached down to pick up his digital stopwatch. Both were hanging from long cords around his neck. He had half a sporting goods store there.

As I waited for him to blow the whistle, I looked at the other end of the court. They were doing some sort of drill over there, but not really. Mostly, they were watching me. I had an audience, and I wasn't even sure what I was supposed to do!

TWEEEEEEET!

I took off dribbling with my right hand and slid between the first and second cone with no problem.

TWEET TWEET!

I looked up and saw the coach pull the whistle from his mouth and yell, "Touch the cone! With your left!"

I was almost past the next cone and looking over at the coach. I reached behind me with my left and swatted for the top of the orange cone. I found it on the second swipe but lost the ball in the process.

TWEET TWEET!

Down at the other end, I heard laughter. What the heck was this drill supposed to prove, anyway, that we could pet dogs while we played hoops? I went back to the starting line.

TWEEEEET!

I slid between the first and second cones. I went a little slower this time, but I swatted the cone right on its pointy head. I sped up a little between the second and third: dribble-dribble-pat-dribble-dribble.

"Good," called Coach B. "Now cross it over!"

I got the dribble and the pat but I ran out of space on the crossover move and bumped the cone.

TWEET TWEET!

Ugh. I think I just got called for charging a cone.

"Kurt," called Coach. "Show him what he's supposed to do."

Kurt walked over to the first cone with a big smirk on his face and put his hands out for the ball. I tossed it to him. Then he lined up and TWEEEEET!

He zipped around the cones, patting them on the tops as he went. Coach called out crossover and he did. Coach called out between the legs, and he did that, too.

Congratulations, I thought. *This is probably the two-hundredth time you've done this drill.* It was the first for me. We didn't waste time on these at tournaments.

Kurt crossed the line after the last cone. There was some clapping from the other end of the court as Coach checked his stopwatch and called out the time. "Like that," he said to me.

I took the ball and got ready. I did a lot better, too. I made it almost all the way around the key before losing the ball again on my second or third crossover.

"All right, that's enough of that," said Coach. I didn't know if he was satisfied with my improvement or just thought I was hopeless. "Let's do some one-on-one."

Finally! I thought. It was about time there was some basketball at this basketball tryout.

"Kurt, you're on defense," said Coach. "Amar'e, you take the ball out up top."

We both headed up to the top of the key. Kurt leaned in and whispered, "This isn't full speed. Nice and easy, so don't sweat it."

That seemed pretty cool of him. Maybe he wasn't such a jerk after all. He checked the ball to me, and I took a few easy dribbles to my right. He came up on me and I ducked my left shoulder toward him, nice and easy, to create a little space. I gave him a quick jab step, and he kind of bit on it. I headed toward the hoop at like 80 percent of my top speed. At that speed, he caught up with me in a few steps. I was thinking of maybe spinning or putting up a hook shot, but right then he shot forward at full speed. He shouldered me aside and grabbed the ball.

"I'll take that," said Kurt, but I noticed he didn't say it loud enough for the coach to hear him.

"What the?" I said. I didn't know if that was a foul, but it definitely wasn't "nice and easy."

"All right, Amar'e," said Coach. "You're on D."

I checked Kurt the ball, and he started out with a few slow, lazy dribbles. I thought about shooting out and stealing the ball myself, but now it seemed like it really was "nice and easy." I kept my guard up, though. I didn't want to be a jerk, but I didn't want to be a chump, either.

Suddenly, Kurt took off at full speed toward the hoop. I managed to stay with him. As soon as he realized he wasn't getting by me, he turned and started backing in toward the hoop. I was pretty sure he was an eighth grader, a full two years older than me, but I hung tough. He took the kind of time he never would've had in a real game and finally put up a hook shot from five feet out. It bounced around and in.

TWEEEET!

"So much for nice and easy," I said.

He walked past me so close that his shoulder brushed against mine. As he did, he whispered something: "You got schooled."

That snake, I thought, but I didn't have time for anything more. Gerry already had the ball, and I was on D first this time.

"This is full speed, right?" I asked as I checked the ball back to Gerry.

He gave me a weird look. "Of course," he said.

Gerry wasn't as tall as Kurt, but he was still pretty big. At least we were both playing at the same speed. He put up a contested shot and it rimmed in. When it was my turn, I did the same thing. I was glad to be on the board.

"Nice shot," said Gerry as it dropped through.

"Thanks, you too," I said.

Coach blew his whistle again, and I wondered what was up next. The answer was nothing, at least not today.

"All right, I've seen enough," he said.

That was it? I thought. I wanted a do-over, but it turned out I didn't need one.

"Welcome to the team, Amar'e," said Coach B. "We'll see you here tomorrow for practice."

I looked over at Kurt, already down at the other end getting high fives from his friends. *What did I just sign up for?*

CHAPTER 6

Junior was home by the time I got back from practice. "How'd it go?" he asked.

"All right," I said. "Took out about half a dozen orange cones, but I made the team."

"What'd they do, give you a driver's test?"

"More like a dribbler's test."

"Oh, yeah, those things are tough the first few times," he said. "Least you made it. That's cool."

"I guess," I said.

"Come on," he said. "You're a baller, STAT. Sixth grade and already on the team . . ."

He gave me a big, toothy smile.

"A baller like my brotha," I said, and I smiled, too.

Dad came home a little later, and Junior was like, "Watch out, Pops. There's a Bear in here!"

Dad jumped back like he was scared. Suddenly, they had me feeling pretty good about things. Mike had said I was representing our grade, all the kids like him who'd be trying out next year. But looking around my house, all three of us smiling now, I knew I was representing my family, too. When my first practice started the next day, I'd be ready.

After dinner, I went out in the driveway, set up some flowerpots, and practiced dribbling. I had been practicing out here for years. Learning how to play with Mike and Deuce, messing around for fun. But now I was on a top school team and I'd be playing indoors.

I caught up with Mike and Deuce the next morning to let them know I'd made the team.

"Cool," said Mike.

"Never had a doubt," said Deuce.

"Hey, you guys want to check out that new ice cream place today?" said Mike. "I'm thinking it'll take ten minutes by bike, tops."

I was halfway through saying "definitely" when it hit me. "I can't today," I said.

"Oh yeah," said Mike. "Forgot about that."

This was definitely going to take some getting used to. As my best friends headed home to grab their bikes at the end of the day, I headed to the gym. The first thing I did was check in with Coach B. He gave me a lock and a practice jersey. I'd seen how everyone was dressed the day before, so I knew to bring my own stuff and throw the practice jersey on over the top. It was definitely a relief to pull on shorts from the right decade, lace up my good high-tops, and throw on my goggles.

I didn't really know anyone when I got to the gym, but at least I looked the part. I had the jersey and the height. Even though I was a year or two younger than the others, I was at least as tall as most of them.

I saw Kurt in one group of kids and Gerry in another. I sort of edged over toward that second group. I figured I'd just try to blend in until I figured things out a little better. Unfortunately, Coach B had other ideas.

TWEEEEEEET!

The whistle got everyone's attention.

"Listen up, everyone," called Coach as he walked toward the middle of the gym. "I want to introduce you to your newest teammate. This is Amar'e."

Everyone was already looking at me. I was the only new guy here, and they'd noticed. I lifted my chin and gave them a quick nod.

"As you know, we fell a game short of our goal last season," the coach continued. "I have no intention of falling short again. Amar'e is young, but he has a lot of experience playing in the weekend tournaments around here. I think he can help put us over the top for that championship."

I know Coach meant well but I really wished he hadn't said that. I saw Kurt lean over and whisper something to his little group, and a few of them started laughing. Coach shut them up with his whistle. I was pretty sure I was going to be hearing that thing in my sleep before long.

"Get the cones!" he shouted.

One after another, the Bears slid through the drill, bopping the tops as they went.

"Crossover!" cried the coach. "Between the legs!"

And they did. It was like watching a military operation. I still wasn't sure how useful this drill would be when it was time for a real game, but there was no doubt these guys were good at it. Every once in a while, one of the bigger guys would lose the ball. Nothing against them, but I was glad. It took some of the pressure off me.

I did pretty well on my first time around. I lost the ball twice, but it didn't get too far away, and I didn't hold things up much. I did better on my second try, and Coach B gave me a little nod as I crossed the line.

"Cones away!" called Coach. "Fast-break drill!"

I liked the sound of that: Who didn't like fast breaks? But as I followed everyone up toward the center of the court, I heard something from the group behind me: "Try to keep up this time, kid."

I looked back, expecting to see Kurt again. But all I saw were unfamiliar faces. I wanted to say something back, but I wasn't even sure who to say it to. Three lines were forming, and I got in the one on my right.

If I wanted to make a statement, this is where I'd have to do it. The drill was pretty simple: There were three lines. The guy in the middle was on defense and the two on the sides were running the break. Of course, simple doesn't mean easy. The first group that went blew by the defender only to brick the layup. The defender made all the right moves in the second group, but the guy hit a tough shot, anyway.

I watched the action closely, and took a few looks at the players I'd be matched up with. They were both from Kurt's group of friends, the ones who'd high-fived him after he'd given me a hard time at the tryout. The defender was named Joe, and everyone called the guy I'd be on offense with Deek.

One more group went, and then it was our turn. Coach blew the whistle, and the defender started back-pedaling fast.

"Shut 'em down, Joe!" someone called.

The coach bounced me the ball, and we were off.

There were two rules on offense: You had to go full speed — I mean, they don't call it a "slow break." And you had to go toward hoop. That was so you couldn't run over to corner, draw the defender with you, and then toss it to the other guy, wide open under- neath. There was only one rule on defense: Don't foul.

I took a quick dribble and then fired the ball over to Deek. A lot of times on the break, the earlier you make the first pass, the more likely you are to get it back. I sprinted toward the hoop as Joe followed the ball and went toward Deek.

Joe stayed there, too. He was on Deek like glue, which allowed me to break into the open on my side. I clapped my hands: Hit me! I was sure we would score now. I could practically see the ball going up and in. But Deek never gave it up. We made eye contact, so I know he saw me. Joe was on him like hair on a dog, but he forced up a fadeaway.

PWAHNK!

He got his shot blocked so hard it bounced off the gym wall. And there I was standing all alone under the basket. *What was that?* I wondered. They didn't even look back at me as they walked back up the court, laughing to each other.

I was on defense next. Coach blew the whistle and Deek started dribbling at top speed toward the hoop. I didn't know if he was a ball hog or if he just hadn't wanted to pass the ball to me last time. But I knew he'd pass it this time. I could tell he and Joe were tight.

I stayed with Deek as he zoomed toward the rim. I could hear Joe's sneakers slapping the court behind me, so I knew more or less where he was. As the space started to run out, I watched for the pass. When Deek one-handed the ball back toward Joe, I was ready. I plucked it right out of the air.

TWEET TWEET!

Our turn was over, but I was alone under the hoop for the second straight time. This time I had the ball. Maybe I shouldn't have, but I guess I wanted to make a point (or two). I rose up and popped in a short jumper.

TWEET TWEEEEET! "Don't hold up the show!" called Coach.

I got the ball and fired it back up court. Then I followed Deek and Joe up the side of the court, so I wouldn't get in the way of the next group coming down. Deek mumbled to Joe, "Show-off."

I headed over to the last line for my second turn on offense. I was pretty sure I wouldn't get a pass this time, either. As I walked to the end of the line, a hand popped out in front of me. It was waist-level, palm out. I looked up and it was Gerry, congratulating me for the stop. I didn't know if he was offering a low five so that no one else would see it, or if that's just what he did. But the way things were going, I'd take it. I reached out and slapped his hand as I passed.

After that, Coach ran through some plays: pick-and-roll, high screen, backdoor cuts. I'd seen those plays before, but the way he talked about it was a lot more precise and detailed than what I was used to on the playground.

"First game's on Friday," yelled the coach. "You all need to have this down by then. One mistake and these plays don't work!"

I could tell from the *there he goes again* looks on their faces that the others had heard this all before. Not me. I listened closely and tried to absorb as many details as I could.

After practice, I volunteered to help get all the balls back into the rack. I was in no hurry to head into that locker room, anyway. By the time I did, it was mostly empty.

Someone had a bunch of books spread out on one of the benches. I was pretty sure they were eighth-grade textbooks. It took me a few seconds to realize it was Deek. A few more people left, and suddenly we were the last two people in there. It was kind of awkward. I thought he might give me more attitude, and I wasn't necessarily in the mood to take it.

But he didn't say a word. He just kept looking at those books. He opened one up, closed it again, pushed it aside, and then picked up another one. He looked stressed out about it.

I grabbed my backpack, heavy with my own books, shut my locker, and got out of there. The last thing I saw as I slipped out the door was Deek stuffing every one of those books back in his locker and slamming the door shut.

CHAPTER 7

"**Y**o, STAT," said Deuce from across the table at lunch. "We gonna see you at the lake?"

"The lake?" I said, and then I remembered. Saturday was one of the big annual cookouts down at Lake Wales. It had some long, corny name, like the Lake Wales Whale of a Lake Lake Bake — like there'd been a sale on the word *lake* or something. As a kid with any self-respect at all, there was no way you'd say it out loud. "Oh, the cookout," I said. "You know it!"

"Well, we better get there before this guy," he said, hooking a thumb toward Mike. And it was true, too. Mike could throw down with food. He'd eat pretty much anything and then ask for seconds. He looked up and, sure enough, his mouth was so full there was sandwich coming out the front of it.

"Who, me?" he said through the food.

We had a good laugh at that.

"Mouth of the south!" said Dougie.

Mike swallowed and said, "Aw, don't worry about me. There's going to be plenty of food there for everyone."

He was right about that. There was always a ton of food at the cookouts down at the lake. Mike got a far-away look in his eyes and started listing them off: "Burgers and hot dogs and barbecue chicken and potato salad. Corn grilled up just the way I like it."

We were all sitting there picturing it right along with him. And then we all looked down and saw our soggy cafeteria sandwiches. Reality bites sometimes. I looked down at my little carton of milk. "And fresh lemonade and iced tea," I said.

Deuce looked over at the so-called brownie on his tray. "And cakes and pies for dessert," he said.

"Stop it, guys," said Mike. "You're killing me!"

"You started it," said Deuce.

"Yeah, but I stopped before I got to the desserts," said Mike. "That's just messed up!" He looked down at his tray, then back up at us. He gave us a shrug like, *What're you gonna do?* Then he popped the dried-up little brownie in his mouth and began to chew.

"Like a hockey puck," he said as he chewed. The brownie paste blacked out his two front teeth.

Now that we'd started talking about the cookout, I was probably looking forward to it even more than Mike. I wasn't as much of a food-seeking missile as he was, but I already missed hanging out with my boys. "Yep," I said, "I'll see you all there."

Thursday was just a good day in general. My friends were in a good mood, and we already had plans for the weekend. And we had the test on the Aztec chapter in history and I crushed it. I even got the extra-credit question.

So I was feeling pretty good when I said so long to Mike and Deuce after last period and headed for the gym. I thought my good day might keep going, and I'd have my first good practice.

Man oh man, was I wrong.

I ducked into the locker room and changed into my shorts and sneakers. I was wearing a T-shirt from one of the really good tournaments I'd been in, and I didn't exactly rush to pull my practice jersey on over it. I was coming to play today. But as soon as I got into the gym, things took a nosedive.

"I've got to take care of something," said Coach B. He didn't say what it was, but he was sporting a coat and tie instead of his usual shorts and neck full of whistles and stopwatches. "The captains will run things until I get back. They know what you need to work on as well as anyone. Just no one get hurt."

I barely even heard those last two sentences. I was thinking: *Oh no, please don't let him be one of the captains*. I looked around for Kurt. As soon as I saw him, he gave me a wicked smile. Then he stepped forward.

"I got this, Coach," he said.

Of course he was. Ugh.

"You too, Mark," said Coach.

Another guy stepped forward. I'd noticed him before. The other kids called him Bibo, which I figured was his last name. He moved like a baller — smooth and easy — and he'd been unstoppable in the fast-break drill. But I'd never heard him say a single word. He let his game do the talking, and I totally respected that. But I knew it wasn't going to help me today.

TWEEEEEEET!

I looked over. I couldn't believe it. Kurt had the whistle, and Coach B was already gone.

"All right, losers!" shouted Kurt. "Free throws! We're not leaving any points at the line tomorrow."

And that's when I realized it. The tone of his voice . . . The way he acted like he should've been in charge all along . . . This guy wasn't just a jerk to me. This guy was just a jerk.

"Eighth graders up here," he said, pointing to one end of the court. "Seventh graders down there," he said, pointing to the other. "Sixth graders, try not to hurt yourself."

Then again, he definitely wasn't my biggest fan.

There was some laughter from the usual suspects. Deek had his fist over his mouth trying to cover it up. (But not trying too hard.)

"You come with me," Kurt said to me once it had quieted down.

Great, I thought as we all headed toward the lines. I was surprised to see Bibo heading down to the other end. He was only in seventh grade?

The drill was downright diabolical. How it worked was that each player had to make four free throws before the next person could go. Everyone counted out each make: "One!" and "Two!" They didn't count the misses, but they sure saw them. I was near the back of the line, and every time I heard "Four!" I got a little more nervous.

This drill was designed to make us nervous, to put the pressure on, just like in a real game. I didn't mind that so much. The problem: I hardly ever shot free throws. On the playground and even at most of the tourneys, foul calls were pretty rare. And most of those just meant you got to take the ball out. Free throws? That wasn't a big part of my game.

"Four!" I heard. I swallowed hard and took another step closer to the front. I guess they were about to be.

They call them free throws, but I would've paid someone to take this set for me. I was second to last in line, so I'd just watched plenty of guys make their four. I pushed my goggles up onto my head for a better look and then did what the other kids had done. I bounced the ball a few times, got a good grip on it, and then bent my knees and kind of squatted down.

I rose up and fired. It felt weird to stay on the ground and not jump. I had a lot more experience with jumpers from this distance than with free throws. Sure enough, without my legs in it, the shot came up short. It clonked off the front rim.

One of the guys bounced the ball back to me. I put a little more oomph into the next one with my arms. I muscled it, and this one clanked off the back rim. At least I was in the neighborhood.

"You just got two shots and missed 'em both," said Kurt.

He'd said the same thing to a few other guys, but it still stung. I didn't even dribble this time, just rose up and drained a jumper.

"One!" a few people called out, but Kurt blew the whistle.

"Doesn't count," he said. "You can't take jump shots from the line."

I wanted to say, "Pretty sure I just did." I dribbled twice, bent my knees, and fired. The ball bounced from the back rim to the backboard and dropped through the hoop.

"One!" everyone called out.

I took a deep breath. Three more to go. The rest of them didn't go much better, but I hit the last two in a row. It felt like maybe I was getting the hang of it, but I was still glad to be done.

Turned out, the kid after me was even worse. He was the biggest guy on the team, but he moved kind of awkwardly. He was probably in the middle of a growth spurt. Those can be tough.

"He's a brick HOUSE!" someone sang after he clanked his third shot in a row. But he was an eighth grader, too, so he had some friends to back him up.

"Don't listen to 'em, Kelvin. You got this."

But he didn't. He clanked nine before he sank four.

"Good thing you two are tall," said Kurt, shaking his head.

I looked over at Kelvin, and he made a funny bug-eyed expression at Kurt's back. I'd done better than him — missed five, made five, if you counted the jumper — but I didn't mind being lumped in with him. At least he had a sense of humor.

"All right, let's run some full court," called Kurt.

I thought the captains might pick teams, but they didn't need to. We had numbers on our practice jerseys and we just went with odds against evens. Both teams ended up with the same number of players. They even had about the same number from seventh and eighth on each, so I guess Coach planned that out when he gave us the jerseys.

I was on the odd team. Coach had given me a choice between Number 1 and Number 39. "Last two left in your size," he'd said, and the choice was pretty obvious.

Gerry was number 13, and we wound up standing next to each other. "Numero uno," he said. "Nice."

"Thanks," I said. "Lucky thirteen!"

"Yeah, right?"

Kurt was on the other team, and Bibo was on ours. We got the better end of that deal. But I wasn't too happy when Kurt handed the whistle off to Joe and named him "permanent ref."

I started off on the bench, but that was cool. There were just a few kids there. I loosened up a little, and just like that I was in the game.

It felt good to run and cut and all that. I got open a few times — like wide open — but no one passed me the ball. I thought Gerry would've, but he was subbed out most of the time I was subbed in. Mostly, I just watched Bibo operate.

He was shredding the defense with that smooth, easy style of his. Most of the time when he had the ball, the even team didn't *even* have a chance. He reminded me of someone. I couldn't quite place it at first. Then he Supermanned straight up to the rim and threw down a dunk, and I knew. It was my friend Jammer.

He reminded me even more of Jammer when he became the first guy to feed me the ball. He was bringing it up the court, even though he was basically a forward. The whole defense was watching him, but he saw me slip behind my defender. He flashed a quick hand signal. Blink and you'd miss it, but I didn't blink. I knew from the day before that the sign meant back-door cut.

I flashed toward the rim, and he fired a one-handed pass that hit me in stride. I laid it in off the glass for an easy two.

Of course, afterward, everyone was like: "What a pass!" and "Did you see that pass?" No mention of the cut or the bucket: It was like I still wasn't on the court. Bibo gave me a little nod, though. I felt good about that.

A minute later, I was back on the bench. I waited my turn, and when I got back in, I decided to be more aggressive. Our point guard was bringing the ball up this time. He held a hand sign up. *Which one was that again?* I thought. Oh yeah, pick-and-roll. I hustled over to set the pick.

Of course, the other team knew that sign, too. Deek saw it and started trying to duck under the screen before I'd even set it. The result: a collision in the lane. We tagged each other's shoulders pretty good.

There was no way it was a foul. We ran into each other: It was a classic no-call. But as soon as Joe blew the whistle, I knew which way the call was going.

"Offensive foul!" he called.

"Our ball," called Kurt. "Good D, Deek!"

A few minutes later, Coach B reappeared. He'd changed into his practice outfit and didn't have to wait to get his whistle back. He had like three more around his neck. He picked one and brought the game to a halt.

"Okay," he said. "I'm glad to see you all still up and running."

I looked around. No one had gotten hurt while he was gone — though my shoulder might disagree.

"Let's wind things down with one last drill," he said. "I need you guys healthy for the game tomorrow."

Then he turned to Kurt and Bibo. "What do you think we should end with?"

Bibo just shrugged, as usual. But Kurt looked over at me and smiled.

"How about free throws?" he said.

CHAPTER 8

All day Friday, my classmates were letting me know they were going to be at the game. It wasn't just my friends, either. Kids I hardly knew were like: "Good luck tonight! I'll be there!"

Now that there was a sixth grader on the team, my classmates wanted to check it out. The problem: I wasn't sure what there would be to check out.

Part of that was Kurt, but not all of it. There were all the guys who wouldn't pass me the ball, the ones who smirked when I messed up and called me a "hotshot" when I did something well. Plus, I was new to the team and might not get much playing time. I knew I had to pay my dues on the bench. Of course, I didn't mention any of that to my classmates. Mostly I just said thanks and hoped for the best. Maybe things would be different in an actual game.

And it was kind of cool, walking around in my shiny new game jersey. I was the only person who had one in my whole grade. Between math and English, I passed a group of older players in the hallway. They nodded at me, and I nodded back. Those guys had all been ice-cold to me in practice, but at least they could recognize their own jersey.

By the time the final bell of the day rang, I was ready to go.

"You cool?" asked Deuce.

"Yeah," I said. An image of me at the line, jump-shooting that free throw, flashed through my mind. "I guess."

"You're gonna rock it," said Mike.

Deuce had a better read on me, though. "It's just like that first tourney," he said. "Remember how you took care of business?"

I smiled. "Thanks," I said, and then hustled down to

the locker room. I didn't even have to ask if they were staying to watch. I knew they'd be there.

I thought the locker room would be really loud, but it was the opposite. Everyone was quiet and focused. Kids were pulling on their game shorts and lacing up their high-tops like they were going to war. Not that you'd wear shorts and sneakers to war, but you know what I mean.

Coach came in and gave us a quick pep talk. The first shout of the day came at the end, when we all shouted at once: "Go, Bears!"

We hustled into the gym, which had been transformed. It didn't look like the plain place where we sweated out gym class anymore. The bleachers were pulled out, and there were signs and decorations hanging from the walls. Everything was in the same green and white as our uniforms.

Reading the signs, it wasn't hard to figure out who we were playing. They said things like: BEAT THE EAGLES, EAGLES ARE FOR THE BIRDS, and GO BACK TO YOUR NEST!

I looked over at the other bench. They had some pretty big birds over there! I wasn't worried. I'd played against bigger players at the tournaments. And I was pumped up now, ready to go.

"Let's go, STAT!" I heard. I recognized my big brother's voice right away, and I looked up to see where he was sitting. Right next to Mike and Deuce. He pointed at me and I pointed back at him. It was cool of him to take some time off from his job for this.

The teams took the court and the first whistle blew. It wasn't Coach providing the lung power this time: It was a real ref with a black-and-white-striped shirt. I watched Mark Bibo rise up and snag the opening tip. We didn't score on the first possession, though. Or the second. The Eagles were playing some tight D.

"They're in zone!" called Coach B. He was waving his arms around so much, giving instructions and reacting to the action, that he kind of looked like an eagle himself.

I just leaned farther and farther forward on the bench, itching to get in on the action. But almost the whole first half went by, and I was still sitting there. I looked over at the coach half a dozen times. I'd do whatever was best for the team, but there were people here to see me play, and I knew I could help out on the court.

Pretty soon there were only two minutes left in the half, and the score was 20–20, like perfect eyesight. Kelvin got fouled hard underneath and got two free throws. He missed both. Coach was so mad, he subbed him out. I leaned forward again, and this time Coach called my name.

I heard some cheers from the sixth graders in the bleachers. "About time!" yelled Mike.

I spent the next two minutes working hard on defense. The other team fed my guy the ball right away. I think they were testing me out, but I contested the shot and got the rebound. I spent my time on offense getting exactly zero touches. I worked my way through traffic and held my hands up for a ball that never came my way.

We took a two-point lead into the locker room, 24–22. But when the second half started up, I was back on the bench. And this time I stayed there. The game stayed tight and the bench got pretty short, with the starters getting almost all the minutes.

I sat on the bench and cheered on my teammates. But I couldn't bring myself to turn around to the crowd. I felt like I was letting down the people who came to see me.

When the air horn went off at the end of the game, we'd scratched out a 42–40 win. I was happy we won, but I didn't feel like I'd had much to do with it. Bibo was the high scorer with 14, and Kurt had scored 8. Me, I had one board, and maybe some splinters from the bench.

I figured I could make one more contribution. I jumped up off the bench and went over to congratulate my teammates. I high-fived Gerry, and when I turned around, Bibo was right there. I reached out and we bumped fists.

"Great game, man," I said.

He gave me a little nod, which I'm pretty sure was Bibo's version of "Thanks a lot."

Kurt was right behind him, talking to Deek and Joe. He wasn't my favorite guy, but he'd had a good game, too. I extended my fist. He looked at it like it was covered in something nasty and left me hanging. As he walked by, I heard him lean in and say something to Deek. It was one word, and just loud enough for me to hear it: "Benchwarmer."

CHAPTER 9

Saturday morning. No, wait, let me try that again: *Saturday morning!* I was definitely ready for the weekend, and this one was going to be good. There was the big cookout at the lake, and I was meeting my friends there. I tossed off the sheets and looked out the window. A nice, sunny day.

Dad was getting ready for work, and Junior was in the kitchen waiting for his waffles to pop up. Sometimes I'd sneak in there and try to grab them from him, but not today. I was skipping breakfast so that I'd be good and hungry for the cookout.

"You headed down to the lake already?" said Dad,

pulling on a green work shirt as he walked into the kitchen. "Don't think it starts yet."

"Nope," I said. "Got one stop to make first. Going to put in an hour or two down at the library."

He nodded. Staying on top of my homework had been my half of the deal when he signed that permission slip. But also, to play on the Bears, Coach B made you keep your grades up. Otherwise you'd get cut. "There you go, STAT," Dad said.

"Teacher's pet," said Junior.

"Dad's not a teacher," I said.

"But I'll teach you!" Dad said, and they both got down into their joke boxing stances.

It was a long walk down to the local library, but it was a short bike ride. I loaded my books and stuff into my backpack and pedaled off into the bright Florida morning.

The place was pretty sleepy when I got there. There was the usual assortment of old-timers camped out by the papers and a few other people on the computers.

"Mornin'," I said to the librarian.

I headed for one of the tables at the back, and was surprised to see another kid there already. I was even more surprised by who it was: Deek. He had those same books from the locker room spread out on the table in front of him.

He had a look on his face like maybe someone was under the table smashing his foot with a hammer. You could tell he didn't hit the books much, and I sort of wondered what he was doing here on a Saturday morning.

I didn't ask because, well, he'd been a jerk to me all week and I didn't want to talk to him. He looked up when I walked by, but he didn't say anything, either. I pulled a chair out at another table and took out my first book.

I started with math, like usual. I didn't start with it because it was my favorite subject. I started with it because it wasn't: Get it out of the way, you know? I'd stayed on top of my homework during the week, but I'd kind of rushed it. There were a few things that I wasn't sure of, and I wanted to make sure I had them down before we moved on. That's the thing about math: That stuff doesn't go away. It's just added to the stuff you're expected to know. It's like building blocks, and if you miss one, it'll catch up with you.

I finished that up pretty quickly. I put my math book back and took out the book we were reading for English. That was my second-favorite subject. I was saving history for last.

I read a few pages and then headed over to look up a few words I wasn't sure of in the big dictionary. On the way back, I looked over at Deek again. He still had all his books open in front of him. His eyes stayed on one for a while, and then flicked to another. That was no way to study. You needed to concentrate on one thing, and then move on to the next. My mom and dad had both taught me that.

"Hey, Deek," I whispered.

He didn't turn around.

I tried it a little louder: "Hey, Deek!"

Still no response, and I know he heard me. We were the only two back here. I shook my head and went back to my book. A few minutes later, he gathered up all his stuff: half a dozen books and a couple sheets of paper, no more than half full of pencil scratches.

Ten minutes after that, my stomach started growling. I gathered up my stuff, too. What was I supposed to do? You can't shush your stomach just because you're in the library. I knew what would shut it up, though. I pushed through the doors, jumped on my bike, and headed for the lake.

I took all the shortcuts and got there in no time. I locked up my bike, dropped a quarter in a rent-a-locker for my books, and went to find my friends. I knew exactly where to look.

A lot of the organizations in town had set up tables: everything from the churches to the Boy Scouts to some of the businesses. That's where the food was, so I knew that's where Mike and Deuce would be. I found them by the Rotary Club table.

"Mrrgurfl," said Mike, which is Mike-ese for "I sure am enjoying this burger."

Deuce was a little more eloquent. "There you are," he said. "You ready for some food?"

My stomach growled loud enough for him to hear it.

"I guess that's a yes," he said.

I looked over the grill: burgers and hot dogs.

"I think I'm going to hold out for some of that chicken I saw on the way in," I said.

"Chrrrkurn?" said Mike, looking around to find it.

An hour later, we were all stuffed — even Mike. There were tons of kids we knew hanging out: Dougie and our other friends Marcus and Tavoris, and Deuce's cousin Timmy and his friends.

"Hey, Timmy," I said. "You bring your football?"

"You know it," he said.

We got a game together and got busy burning off some of that food. The wide receivers were a little wider after all those burgers and dogs. And I seriously reconsidered that extra helping of mac and cheese when I was trying to cover Dougie on a fly route. It was a good game, though. There were touchdowns, passes, and some long runs for both sides. The defense stiffened up toward the end, but I went up high to haul in a pass from Timmy in the end zone.

"That was a nice grab," Mike said as we sat around on one of the picnic benches afterward.

"Nice to have someone actually pass to me," I said.

"Yeah, what was that all about?" said Deuce. "What were you in the game for yesterday, like a minute?"

"It's not about the playing time," I said, "I just wish they'd look for me when I'm open."

"Yeah, you were wide open a few times," said Mike. "That was lame."

"I felt bad for the people who came to see me."

"Yeah, well, they'd probably heard about the permission slip and the special invitation and all that," said Mike. It was pretty obvious he was talking about himself. "So they thought you'd be in there."

"Yeah," I said, wondering just how many people he'd told that part to.

"I just think it's crazy that they're not letting you do your thing," said Deuce. "That game was too close to have you sitting on the bench."

I didn't really want to talk about it. I wasn't big on complaining, but these were my best friends, and I wanted to be honest about it. "It's just frustrating," I said. "I feel like they're not even giving me a shot. It's like Coach brought me in this year, but the team just wants me to wait till next year, anyway."

Deuce looked over at me and shrugged. "I don't know," he said. "Maybe you should."

"Yeah," said Mike. "We'll all be there next year. It'll be a whole new ball game!"

It was quiet for a while. We were all thinking the same thing. It would definitely be better next year, and I could hang out and have fun with them until then. I looked at both of them. I'd had more fun in this one day than I'd had in a week's worth of practice.

I thought about it and shook my head. "I'm no quitter," I said. "I'll be a good teammate even if they're not. That's just me."

"It's not quitting if you're going back next year," said Deuce. "It's timing, like stepping back before you start your drive."

I let out a little laugh. He could make anything sound reasonable. "Man, D. You should go into politics."

"Or coaching," said Mike.

"Naw," I said. "All his best players would be taking the year off."

They let it drop after that. Mike stood up, ready for round two. "Hey, guys," he said. "Anyone else hungry?"

I left the cookout with a lot to digest, and I don't mean the food. I thought about what Deuce said for the rest of the weekend: timing. I knew part of that was just those two wanting me to hang out with them. But there was something to it, too.

I spent Sunday helping Dad out with a job. Weekends were busy for his lawn-care company, and I was an ace with the push mower. But I guess I was still pretty distracted, because I pushed that mower right through the corner of a flower bed. It was a petunia massacre.

"Whoa, whoa, whoa!" shouted Dad as he dropped his clippers and came running.

It was all over by the time he got there. I'd hit the kill switch on the mower, and the last chewed-up purple petals floated limply to the ground.

"Sorry, Pops," I said. "Just thinking about some things."

CHAPTER 10

I trudged to practice after the final bell on Monday. Basketball had always been fun before, but it felt like a battle lately. Deuce's words were still ringing in my ears, but I tied my sneakers with grim determination.

Turned out, Coach B wasn't in any better of a mood than I was. He was "not satisfied" with our "low-energy" performance at the game on Friday. He said we were "lucky to win" and seriously questioned if we were "getting enough sleep." I wanted to raise my hand and tell him I was getting plenty of rest, since the team wouldn't let me do anything, thanks.

On the plus side, we ran full court for the whole second half of practice. I even managed to get my hands on the ball a few times. The other kids on Team Odd passed it to Gerry, and sometimes Gerry passed it to me.

He hit me with a bounce pass early on. I honestly think it surprised my defender. It was like it hadn't even occurred to him that someone might involve me in the offense. That gave me all the space I needed to drive down the lane. Kelvin was lurking underneath the rim. He was as good at blocking shots as he was bad at free throws, so I had to shake him.

I launched into the same spin move I'd scored with at the tournament, but things went differently this time.

TWEEEEEET!

"That's a travel, Amar'e," called Coach B. "Even ball."

Huh? I gave Coach a look, like; *Since when is that a travel?* It was the exact same move I'd done at the tourney, I was sure of it. But Coach wasn't even looking anymore. I did my best to shake it off and get my head back in the game.

I also got my hands on the ball by crashing the boards at both ends for rebounds. A few minutes later, I hauled in an offensive rebound. There was some traffic down low, but I was pretty sure I could go right back up with it. I took a few dribbles, shifted the ball over, and took a few more.

TWEEEEET!

"That's a carry," barked Coach B. "You palmed it. Even ball."

Did I seriously just get whistled for palming? I'd never seen that called in the tourneys I'd been to — and I'd been to plenty. I just shook my head. The other players freezing me out was one thing, but Coach? All I could do was head back on D.

The next time I got the ball, I tossed it straight to Bibo and let him operate. Sure enough, he shook Kurt with some fancy dribbling and then drained a fadeaway. Coach never whistled him for anything.

Once practice was over, I was, too. I'd had just about enough of this team. But there was someone else I needed to talk to about this, someone else I'd made a commitment to.

I helped clear the plates away after dinner and then said, "Hey, Dad. Got a minute?"

Dad always had time for me when it was serious. "Sure, STAT," he said. "What's up?"

"It's the basketball team," I said.

Dad nodded. "Yeah, Junior told me it wasn't exactly your game."

"I don't think the next one on Wednesday will be any better."

"Why's that, now? Seems like they were pretty eager to sign you up."

"Yeah, exactly, but since then it's like they've been piling on top of me. The other kids almost never pass me the ball, one captain's a jerk, and the other one never talks, and —"

I had more to say, but Dad put up his hands in a stop sign. "Let's start there, okay? Why do you think the other kids don't pass to you?"

"'Cause they're freezing me out? Because they don't want me on the team?" I said. I was mostly just guessing.

"Or, what else might it be?"

I thought about it. "Because I'm new, maybe? Because they've been practicing together for a few weeks and a lot of them know each other already."

"Right," said Dad. "So say you're an eighth grader and you see two players with their hands up. One is your buddy who you played with all last season, and the other is some sixth grader who just showed up yesterday. Who are you going to pass to?"

"Okay, maybe," I said. I could see his point. I needed to prove myself. But how was I supposed to do that if they never gave me the chance?

"And this captain, is he just a jerk to you, or is he a jerk to everyone?"

"He's a jerk to everyone," I said. He'd really been letting Kelvin have it at practice today. "Except his friends."

"Well, even jerks have friends — and you don't want to be one of them. And the other captain?"

I knew where he was going now. "He doesn't talk much to anyone, so it's not like he's freezing me out. . . . But the coach!" I said, bringing out my main point. "I finally got my hands on the ball today and he whistled me for a bunch of things."

Dad didn't look too impressed, and I couldn't understand that. We'd both sat back down at the kitchen table by now, and he leaned back a little in his chair. "Like what?"

"Traveling," I said. "And palming. I've never been called for palming before in my life."

"But did you?" said Dad.

"What?"

"Did you carry the ball?" He made the motion with his hand: a few phantom dribbles, turning his hand over a little, and then a few more dribbles.

"I don't know," I said. "I guess I might've. But who calls that?"

"Coaches call that," said Dad, and then he broke into a little smile. "And every once in a blue moon a ref."

I sat there thinking about it, and he let me. For a while, the only sound in the kitchen was the hum and occasional flicker of the overhead light.

"Listen, STAT," Dad said after a minute or two. "I know you think they're busting your tail, and they probably are. But you have to think of why they're doing it. You can't fix something until you know why it isn't working."

The kitchen light flickered again, like it was agreeing. Dad looked up at it, probably wondering where he'd put the replacement bulb.

"Thanks, Pops," I said. "I think I know what I need to do."

I looked out the window. It was still light out.

"You got it," said Dad. "Now go get Junior. He can help you with a lot of this."

I suddenly remembered something my big brother had said at the tournament the weekend before: *You know you traveled, right?*

"Yeah," I said with a smile. "If there's one guy I can count on, it's him."

We did kind of a side hug, just because. Then I headed off to get my basketball and drag my older bro out into the driveway before it got too dark to practice.

CHAPTER 11

*H*eading to practice felt a lot different on Tuesday. I even talked a little as I was changing in the locker room. "It's gonna be a good day," I said to Gerry as he laced up his sneakers down the bench from me.

"Hope so," he said.

But I was sure of it. I just had to remember two things. First, special invitation or not, I was still the new kid. I had to prove myself to the team. Second, basketball was fun. I couldn't let the negative stuff drag me down.

As I headed toward the door, Bibo was just in front of me. I said something I'd been meaning to for a few days: "Hey, man. Your fadeaway is lethal."

I thought he'd just nod, like usual, but he actually answered. "Thanks," he said. Okay, it was just one word, but come on: That was like a major speech for him.

Practice started out with that same dribbling drill. But you know what? It was actually fun, if you didn't put too much pressure on yourself. Now that I thought of it, it kind of reminded me of the obstacle course my friends and I used to run for fun back in the day at the park.

The whistle blew and I took off. Every time I had to pat the top of a cone I thought, *Take that, conehead!* I made it through clean, in a pretty good time. I was even kind of disappointed when we didn't run it again.

We did a few more drills and then what I'd been waiting for: full court, odds versus evens. Two guys were out sick today. What were the odds they'd both be odds, I thought, but they were. That meant we had no bench, and I knew I'd be in the whole game.

I got the ball right off the tip, but I didn't get greedy. I did the right thing and fired it up the court to our point guard, an eighth grader named Isaac. I didn't have to wait long to get it back. On the next possession, Gerry drove to the hoop. He drew the D and then dished the ball to me along the baseline. I had a clean look and drained the short jumper. Gerry and I low-fived as we headed back up the court. I was officially on the board!

A few minutes later, I came up with a loose ball near midcourt. Out of the corner of my eye, I saw Bibo's long, lean frame break away from the swarm of players. I tossed a quick lead pass over the top. He scooped it up and had only one guy to beat. He faked him out of his sneakers and dunked it.

After that, Bibo returned the favor. We had the ball near the top of the key. My guy was playing off me because he wasn't expecting Isaac to pass it to me. I wasn't, either, to be honest. But as Bibo worked his way through traffic, he said his second word of the day. "One!" he called out.

At first, I thought maybe that was a play, maybe something they'd worked on before I joined the team. I realized he meant my jersey number a second before my defender did, and bolted toward the rim. Isaac scrunched up his face, like: *Really?* But he did what the cocaptain said and launched a chest pass my way.

It was almost an easy two, but Kurt got his finger on the pass at the last second and deflected it just enough. I had to stutter-step as I hauled it in, and that gave Kelvin enough time to get back into position underneath. I launched into my spin move, but this time I was careful not to take the extra step. Kelvin swatted for the ball but got more of me than of it. This time, I was glad to hear the whistle blow.

"Two shots!" called Coach B.

I headed to the line and tried to remember the tips Junior had given me, not just about how to stand but also how to breathe and shoot. "Relaxed and smooth," he'd said. I repeated those words in my head as I drained the first free throw. That put us up by two, but my second shot rimmed out.

I passed Kurt on my way back up the court. "Nice D," I said. That was more advice from my brother: "Kill 'em with kindness." It was true, anyway — I had no idea how he got his hand on that pass. A look of total confusion flashed across his face before turning into the angry scowl I was used to.

Kelvin wasn't happy, either. I think going right at him like that made the big guy mad. He muscled his way to the hoop and powered one home to tie the score. Coach B blew the whistle. He liked to end the scrimmages when they were tied, and I guess that made sense.

When the whistle blew, I got nods from Bibo and Isaac, and a high five from Gerry. We finished practice with some sprints. Afterward, Gerry and I were bent over, trying to get some air back into our lungs. He looked over and huffed, "You were right, you know."

"About what?"

"It was a good day."

I straightened up: "It's not over yet."

"It is for me," he said.

As he headed for the locker room, I headed in the other direction.

"Coach B?" I said.

"What is it, Amar'e?"

"Mind if I take some foul shots? I'll put the balls away when I'm done."

He broke into a big smile. "Did you know those are just about a coach's favorite words?"

As I headed toward the line, I heard someone else call out behind me. "Yo, Coach, mind if I join him?" I recognized the voice.

"Kelvin," said Coach, "I would be *delighted*."

So he and I spent a good half hour out there, taking free throws and rebounding for each other. We didn't say much, but I passed along some of my brother's advice.

"Relaxed and smooth," said Kelvin. "I like that."

At one point toward the end, he hit three in a row.

CHAPTER 12

Wednesday was an away game, and that meant my first bus trip as part of the team.

In homeroom, Deuce warned me to sit in the front and watch out for pranks. Sometimes the team would "have a little fun" with the new guy.

Still, I climbed aboard that big yellow bus not really knowing what to expect. The answer: a whole lot of noise. The team was turned up to maximum volume because Coach wasn't on the bus yet. It was fun to be on a school bus for something other than school. The players were joking and shouting across the aisle at each other.

As I waded into the craziness, the first thing I had to figure out was where to sit. I'd had one decent practice, but that didn't mean all that freeze-out-the-new-kid stuff had vanished. Gerry was already sitting with someone, but I found another seatmate in the row ahead who wouldn't complain.

I sat down next to the big ten-gallon water cooler we kept at the end of the bench during games. Gerry leaned forward in his seat to say hi. Then he introduced me to the guy sitting next to him, a seventh grader named Anton.

"And this is Water Cooler," I said. "He's kind of quiet, but it's okay. He's cool."

"Yeah, we met last game," said Anton. "He says even less than Bibo."

As we were laughing, the bus suddenly got quiet. That's how I knew Coach had climbed aboard. He wasn't alone, either.

"Listen up!" he shouted. "This is your 'adult chaperone' for the trip. His name is Mr. Cromartin, but you guys from last year know what he goes by."

"Hey, Sarge!" called Kelvin. A little ripple of laughter spread through the bus.

A quick look at his buzz cut and straight, stiff back told the rest of us that Sarge was short for Sergeant. He marched down the aisle and plunked down next to an unsuspecting eighth grader three-quarters of the way back.

"So much for any pranks," I said under my breath.

Things settled down once the bus started moving. People mostly just talked or looked out the windows. Every once in a while, Coach would turn around and half stand in his seat. Then he'd shout back with something we needed to remember or watch out for during the game.

"East Lake is always a big running team," he called. "We need to get back, back, back on D!"

That sounded good to me — I loved to get up and down the court!

I wasn't spying or anything, but Deek and Isaac were sitting in the seat ahead of me. I was close enough that I heard a lot of what they were saying.

"How're the grades, man?" said Isaac.

Deek shook his head. "Not good, man."

"I thought you were gonna get that sorted out."

"I've been trying!" he said. "I've got too much stuff to make up. It's like I don't even know where to start."

"Not good," said Isaac. "You gotta get that figured out before report cards. You're too good, man. We can't lose you."

"Thanks, man," said Deek. "I'm trying."

My mind flashed back to all those books spread out in the locker room. I remembered him folding up those few half-full pages and leaving the library. All of a sudden, I knew what it meant. Deek was going to fail off the team! He hadn't said one nice word to me yet, but I still felt kind of bad for him.

A few minutes later, the bus pulled up at the school. Everyone started buzzing again. Not even Sarge could keep the bus quiet when we saw the hand-painted sign out front: GO, LAKERS! BEAT THE BEARS!

"Oh, it's on!" said Isaac.

"The Lakers are going down!" someone shouted from the back of the bus.

We were all fired up by the time the bus pulled to a stop alongside the gym. We poured off the bus and headed straight into the gym. The other team was warming up, and there was already a crowd in the bleachers. It looked to be about half students and half parents. They booed us big-time as we entered, but that only hyped us up. Some people had made the trip to support us, too, but there were too few of them to match the hoots of the home crowd.

"Nobody boos the Bears!" bellowed Kelvin.

We warmed up quickly with some stretching and layup lines and things like that. The crowd booed our makes and cheered our misses. I was as revved up as anyone, and that made it tough to start off on the bench. But I had a lot of energy to root for the guys who were on the court.

And it was a good game to watch. Coach wasn't kidding: The Lakers were run-and-gun from the opening tip. They were hoisting up shots five or ten seconds into the shot clock — and we were starting to do the same thing. That stuff is contagious. It's just so much fun to play that way, and our energy level was through the roof. But Coach wasn't happy.

He called an early time-out and then started chewing out the starters. "I said get back fast on defense!" he

said. "I didn't say to rush shots on offense." He was looking straight at Isaac, because he was the point guard.
"We still need to run our plays and get good looks."

To make sure everyone got the point, he benched
Isaac and Deek. He put Gerry in to run the point.

"Let's go, Gerry!" I said, and gave one big clap.

"You too," said Coach.

I looked around to see who he meant.

"Wait, *me*?" I said.

"Can you keep it under control? Maybe look for that
pick-and-roll?"

"Yes, sir!"

"Then get in there!"

The time-out ended. Bibo, Kurt, and Kelvin headed
back to the court. And Gerry and I went right along with
them. We bumped fists as we ran. Now, this was a com-
bination I could deal with.

CHAPTER 13

We inbounded the ball and headed up the court. The first possession played out about how you'd expect. Coach had just chewed the starters out for hoisting up quick shots, so you can bet we spent a good chunk of the clock passing the ball around the outside: Gerry to Kurt to Bibo to me. I saw Kelvin backing his guy in down low and passed it to him, but he just passed it back out to Bibo.

When Bibo passed it over to Gerry, I thought: Here we go again. But they knew what they were doing. Gerry faked another pass to Kurt, but then turned and whipped it back to Bibo. His defender was half hypnotized by all the slow-mo passing. He barely even reacted as Bibo rose up and drained an uncontested jumper.

"Way to work it!" called Coach. He was happy: time off the clock and points on the board. That was his style.

We all hustled back on defense as they inbounded the ball underneath. Making shots was also a great way to slow down the Lakers' fast break. We got in good position and were able to kind of bog them down on the next possession. Now they were the ones passing the ball around.

My guy tried to back me in, but I held my ground. I was thinking, *Now that I'm in the game, you're going to have to bump me harder than that!* Instead, he passed it back out. Kurt's guy wound up launching a long jumper. Kelvin and I worked to get position. When the ball clanged off the rim, I got a hand on it and tipped it to him.

On the way up the court, Gerry looked at me and said, "Be ready." He didn't need to say for what. Coach had said it during the time-out: pick-and-roll. I set the screen on Gerry's defender near the free throw line, then rolled to the hoop with my hand up in the air.

Gerry turned and looped a pass to me. I hauled it in and turned to size up the traffic down low. There were too many bodies to chance it, so I lofted up a floater in the lane.

Nothin' but net, baby! Man, I loved the pick-and-roll.

Kurt took the shot himself on each of our next two possessions. I think he was feeling a little left out of things. He scored on the first. I'll admit it was a nice step-back move. But he bricked a long jumper on the trip after that. The long rebound led to a fast-break bucket for the Lakers.

Coach made more substitutions after that. Kurt, Gerry, and I were out. Isaac and Deek came back in, along with Joe.

"All right," said Coach as we came out of the game. I guess that was as much as we were going to get, but I felt pretty good. I'd scored and done my part on D. Plus, we'd done a good job of slowing things down and getting quality shots. Gerry and I headed over to see my favorite seatmate, Water Cooler. Kurt cut in front of us, of course. Gerry and I just looked at each other and rolled our eyes.

I was hoping I'd go right back in, but I didn't. The game stayed close, and the starters got most of the time. When Coach did substitute, it was mostly eighth graders. I finally got a few more minutes in the second half. I hauled in an offensive rebound, and scored on the putback. That stretched our lead from two to four, and we wound up winning by six.

It wasn't exactly a blowout, but it was better than the last game — and against a better team. It was better for me, too. It was just a couple buckets and a couple boards, but it was something. Plus, we shut down the crowd that was booing us.

We lined up to slap hands with the other team. It was weird that I got more "good games" from them than from our own eighth graders, but whatever. At least Kelvin came over and said, "Three-for-five!" He meant his free throws. He'd been something like one-for-six the game before, and we both smiled as we bumped fists.

We piled back onto the bus and headed home. We all took pretty much the same seats, so I was between Gerry and Anton and Deek and Isaac, with my "cool" friend next to me. (The water cooler was a lot more popular on the trip home.) About a mile into the trip, I decided it was time to switch up seats.

"Can't believe I have to do homework when I get back," I heard Deek grumble.

"Yeah, you better," said Isaac.

I leaned over the top of the seat. "Yo, Isaac," I said. "Could you switch with me for a minute?"

He looked back at me like I had glow-in-the-dark bugs crawling out of my ears. Neither one of them had said a word to me after the game — even though it was Isaac's miss I'd cleaned up on that put-back.

Finally, Deek shrugged. "Whatever," he said.

Isaac got up and we swapped seats quickly. The bus driver and the Sarge both shouted at us at the same time. But by the time Coach turned around, we were both sitting down in our new seats, acting like nothing had happened.

I knew I didn't have much time, so I got right down to it. "No offense, man, but you're doing it wrong."

"Doing what wrong?" he said, his eyes narrowing.

"Studying," I said.

He looked a little shocked, maybe even angry. For a second, I seriously thought I'd gone too far. His shoulders were tensed up like he was mad. But then they dropped. "You're probably right," he said. "There's so much homework this year. I'm getting crushed."

"Yeah, I've seen you spread out all those books and just, like, look at 'em. You've got to divide and conquer."

"Divide?" he said. "You mean my math homework?"

"No, all of it," I said. "You've got to focus on one subject at a time and check things off your list."

I waited to see if he was still with me. He nodded, so I went on.

"Say you've got homework in three subjects — not just reading, but stuff you've got to hand in. You can look at it all and get kind of overwhelmed, right?"

He nodded again.

"Right, so just do the first thing. Doesn't matter which, but I like to save my favorite subject, or maybe just the easiest assignment, for last. Anyway, you just take out what you need for that one subject, and you power through."

The light came halfway on in his eyes. "And then you've only got two subjects left," he said.

"Right, and the last one is the easiest!"

"So it's not one big mess."

"Yeah, it's just a few, you know, small messes."

"Hmm," he said.

I waited for something more, but he just looked down at his feet and said "Hmm" again.

"Sarge isn't looking," hissed Isaac from behind us. "Switch back!"

So we did. I didn't know if what I'd said to Deek had sunk in — or if it would even work for him — but I hoped so. I tried to imagine what it would feel like to flunk off the team. I wouldn't wish that on anyone.

By the time I settled back into my seat, everyone on the bus was talking about something else. The next game. It was the biggest one yet, they were saying, maybe the biggest of the whole season. It was against the Central Cougars.

"What's so big about Central?" I said to Gerry.

"For real?" he said, looking surprised. "They're the ones who beat us for the title last season."

"When's the game again?" I said.

"Wednesday night, at home."

A home game — the gym packed with our families and friends, and against our biggest rivals. I told myself right then, I'd be ready.

CHAPTER 14

*T*he next few practices should've been sponsored by the local hardware store, because it was all drills, drills, drills on Thursday and Friday. After a few games, Coach already had a long list of things we needed to work on.

"We were shooting it way too fast," Coach told us on Thursday. "We need to work on our passing!"

And he had drills for that. There was one called the extra-pass drill that, well, you can probably figure that out.

"The Lakers were shooting way too fast," Coach told us on Friday. "We need to work on our defense."

Want to bet he had drills for that, too? Some of them we'd done before, and some of them were new to me.

Either way, I did my best to stay focused (not the easiest thing on a Friday afternoon) and worked hard. I knew what Dad would say: that these drills were making me better. And now that I'd had a little playing time, I wanted more.

Kurt and some of the other eighth graders were just as stone-cold to me as always. Maybe even more, now that I'd been subbed in for a few of them. I broke up one of Kurt's passes on the fast-break drill. "Good luck getting your hands on any passes from the bench," he said as we headed back up the court.

But all he could do was make nasty comments. That's the good thing about those drills. We're lined up and everyone gets a turn — and then about eight turns more!

And just like that, it was the weekend. Yes!

I started this one off the same way as the last one. I definitely didn't start every weekend this way, but I had a hunch. I biked over to the library, said hello to the librarian, and headed toward the back. Sure enough, there was Deek. He looked up and saw me. He held up a book. It was the only one he had on the table. I nodded and took a seat at the same table. It definitely wasn't something I would've done a week ago, but he just moved his stuff over to make room.

We sat there for a solid hour. We didn't say much, just worked. Sometimes that helps, though, just having someone else sitting next to you and working, too.

This time, I left first. Deek had already swapped out his books twice by then. As I got up, he put down his pencil. The page he was working on was almost full. He saw me looking and turned it over: The other side was full, too.

"Nice!" I whispered. We bumped fists for the first time, and I was gone.

There was no cookout at the lake today — I wish — but I was way overdue to hang out with Mike and Deuce. We had big plans for today, too — racing our bikes down at the park.

I pedaled fast to get there. I zoomed into the old parking lot and slammed on the brakes, fishtailing to a stop a few feet from where Mike and Deuce were leaning over their handlebars.

"What's up?" I said.

"Waiting for you," said Deuce.

"That's only fair," I said. "Since I'll be waiting for you two after I cross the finish line."

"In your dreams!" said Mike.

We were all smiling. We knew the races would be close. Deuce was small and fast, and could make quick turns on his bike. Mike was big and had raw power. I had some of both: speed and power.

"Let's get to it," said Deuce. He pointed his thumb over his shoulder at his backpack. "I've got everything we need for the course right in here."

We got off our bikes and started building the course. There were empty soda bottles to zip in between, a Frisbee to circle around, and a few other things. The obstacles were my idea.

"We haven't done this in years," said Mike as he positioned a plastic bottle on the pavement. "What made you think of it?"

"Got the idea at basketball practice," I said.

"Cool. So how'd that last game go?" said Mike.

"Not too bad," I said.

"Yeah, that's what you said Thursday," said Deuce. "But, like, how not bad?"

"Just, I don't know, not too bad," I said. "I got a few more minutes, scored some points."

"So, you're happy about it?" said Deuce.

"Not really," I admitted. "But it's getting better. I think some of the other players are starting to realize I'm there."

"So you're gonna stick with it?" said Mike.

That's what this was about. I was wondering what they were getting at. They were still thinking about that "timing." I let them know right away that that train had left the station.

"Yeah," I said. "All I need is a chance to show what I can do. I just need to wait — and work."

"All right, cool," said Mike. The course was done, and we climbed back on our bikes.

"Yeah, cool," said Deuce.

And that was the great thing about my friends. Sure, they wanted to hang out with me more. But they also had my back, no matter what I did. If I had any doubt about that, it vanished a little while later.

"I've got one more piece of equipment in my back-pack," said Deuce after a few good races through the course. "You're closest, STAT. Can you grab it for me?"

I pedaled over to his bag and picked it up. The top flopped open. There was one thing left in there: a basketball.

A big, goofy grin spread over Deuce's face. "Sort of figured you'd stick with it," he said. "Thought you might want to work on some things in, you know, a friendlier environment."

I got a big, goofy grin of my own. The park's basket-ball court was a short ride away. "Hope you guys like free throws," I said.

CHAPTER 15

*T*here was an electric charge at practice on Monday. "Two days till revenge!" bellowed Coach as we filed into the gym. "Those Cougars took the title — our title! — last year. On Wednesday, we let them know we're taking it back!"

He was as fired up as I'd ever seen him, and that got us all fired up, too. We were going to seriously declaw those Cougars! There was one problem. There might have been electricity in the air, but there was jerk-icity on the court. Kurt gave me trouble all practice.

He was eyeballing me any time I did anything, and making little digs and comments. Coach put him in charge of wind sprints at the end of practice and he made me do extras because he said I left early — but everyone left early!

After practice, I got a call from my friend Jammer. He was just checking in, but I knew he was on his school team, too, so I told him about it. He knew the deal right away.

"Guy like that, been on the team a couple of years and now he's captain," said Jammer. "He thinks he runs the place."

"Sounds like him," I said.

"Right, and here you come, a new kid, starting to get some minutes and get some attention. He'll tell people — he probably even tells himself — that you haven't put in the time yet. That you don't deserve it. But really . . ."

"But really he wants to keep it all for himself," I said.

"Yeah, for him and his friends."

Jammer had never met Kurt, but he had him figured out. "You ever have a guy like that on your team?" I asked.

"Man, STAT, I think everyone does at some point."

"So what did you do?"

"I did what I do, man!"

I laughed. What Jammer did was score points by the dozen.

"How's it going for you so far?" he asked.

"Better," I said. "But not good enough. I'm getting some minutes, some buckets."

"Yeah, sometimes you've got to ease your way in," he said. "But that's not you. You've got to get out there and *operate*, STAT. Once you show them what you can do — what you can really do — there won't be anything more to say."

He was right: enough of this a-point-here-and-there stuff. I showed up at practice on Tuesday ready to go. But as soon as I stepped into the gym, I knew there was trouble. Coach was in a suit and tie again, just like before. I got there just in time to see him hand the whistle off — to Kurt.

"Where the heck does he go in that suit?" I said to Gerry as Coach hustled out the door.

"I heard he's buying a house," he said. "Meetings and paperwork and all that."

I pictured Coach sitting in front of a desk down at the bank, his old clipboard full of forms to fill out instead of plays.

"Check out Mr. Bander," said Gerry, pointing over to the far corner. A teacher I didn't know had the first row of bleachers pulled out and was sitting there grading papers.

"He should run practice," I said.

"Old Bander's just here to make sure we don't break anything. I don't think he knows a single thing about hoops."

I looked over at Kurt. "He should still run it," I said.

TWEEEEEEEEEEEEEEEEEEEEEEEEET!

Kurt blew the whistle long and loud. The teacher didn't even look up from his grading. "Enough joking around!" shouted Kurt. "We have one day to practice till the biggest game of the season. Let's get to it!"

Kurt's friends and some of the other kids whooped, and then, sure enough, we got to it. I don't know if he thought he was sticking it to me by starting with free throws. He hadn't bothered to stick around and see me working on them after practice. But he got the news now.

"One!" shouted the rest of the line as I drained the first one.

"Two!" Kurt looked confused.

"Three!" Kurt looked annoyed.

"Four!" Kurt looked angry. I could practically see the wheels turning behind his eyes, coming up with something worse.

Kelvin went after me and hit his four in six attempts, his best yet. "Yeah, Big Man!" someone called out from the line.

Bibo went next. Coach had given him a whistle, too, but it hung around his neck completely unused. He did his part for the team by demonstrating some silky smooth precision at the line.

"Four!" some joker called out after Bibo hit his first.

Kurt had seen enough. "Full court!" he called. "Odds against evens."

He named Joe permanent ref again, but I knew he wasn't done yet. I knew because he was looking right at me.

"Seventh and eighth only," he said.

That left exactly one person out: me. I'd had enough. "That's ridiculous," I said.

He smirked. "You need to watch and learn, new guy," he said. "Just grab a seat over by Bander."

The old man looked up at the sound of his name and then right back down. But I didn't move.

"Take a seat," said Kurt.

"What a joke," said Gerry.

Kurt cut him a quick look. I appreciated Gerry sticking up for me, but I knew Kurt wouldn't care. He was a good player, but he wasn't a starter, and he was still in seventh.

"You can take a seat, too," said Kurt. "You can just stay on the bench."

The gym was dead quiet now, and every word carried. I looked over at Gerry and gave him a quick nod: *Thanks.*

"All right, the rest of you get out there," said Kurt.

Most of the team jogged toward the center for the tip: most, but not all.

"Nah, I don't think so," said a big voice next to me. "Like the little guy said, this is a joke."

I looked over at Gerry. He didn't mind being called a little guy — to Kelvin almost everyone was little. Kurt's jaw just about hit the floor. He was either totally surprised or just trying to figure out how the even team was going to get by without their center.

"Come on, Kelvin," he said after a few seconds. "This isn't about you. You've put in your time."

The next surprise came from right next to Kurt: from his own group.

"Yeah, you know, I think he's right."

It was Deek. He'd said "I think he's right" instead of "I think you're wrong," but he'd made his point.

"What is this?" said Kurt. "Come on, D-man, you messin' with me?"

Deek shook his head.

"Okay, cool," said Kurt, shaking the surprise off his face. "You can all sit out. We'll run fours."

"Better make it threes," said Isaac. "And good luck running the point."

TWEEEEEEEEEEET!

Kurt looked down at the whistle, still hanging flat against his jersey. Then he swallowed hard and looked over at the only other whistle in the room. We all did.

"Five on five, odds versus evens, the end," said Bibo.

Now it was my jaw that just about hit the floor. It was the longest thing I'd ever heard Mark Bibo say.

And the best.

CHAPTER 16

Game Day. No, wait: *Big-Game Day!* This is what I was picturing back when I handed in that permission slip. I was wearing my new Bears jersey, high-fiving the other players as we passed in the hallway. Kids I didn't even know wished me luck. From what I heard, just about the whole school planned to go to the game.

It wasn't the first time I'd worn the jersey to school for game days, but it was the first time I really felt like a part of the team when I did. It's not like I doubted my skills or anything. I just wasn't sure they wanted me there. But after those guys stuck up for me at practice the day before, I knew.

I think even Kurt and Joe figured it out, because we'd had a good game of five-on-five. There were no cheap fouls, and no hard ones, either. By the time Coach B showed up at the end and took his whistles back, it really didn't seem to matter that much.

Now all that mattered was this game. We were as prepared as we were going to get, and all that was left was waiting for it to start. It felt like it took forever.

I tried to concentrate during classes and then joked around with Mike and Deuce between them. "I wish you guys were playing, too," I told them on our way to lunch.

"We'll be there next year," said Mike.

"Yeah, don't sweat it," said Deuce. "Just warn 'em we're coming. It's only fair!"

They were cool about it, and that made it easier. They were the guys I'd learned to play hoops with — before the tournaments, before the team, before everything. They were the one thing that was missing from all this, I told myself. But even as I thought that, I knew there was something else. I wasn't exactly sure what it was. I could feel it there, like a missing tooth, but I couldn't put my finger on it.

By the time we filed into the cafeteria and found our other friends, I'd forgotten all about it. Eventually, the day crawled over the finish line, and I was changing for the game. The locker room was electric with anticipation and nerves.

And it didn't just feel different; it was different. A huge shadow fell over me as I was lacing up my sneakers. I looked up and there was Kelvin. "You ready, man?" he said.

I reached up and we bumped fists. "You know it!" I said.

A few minutes later, Isaac did the same thing. The silent treatment was officially over. Before he walked away, I added a quick, "Thanks, man."

I didn't have to say for what. Taking my side against Kurt was a big thing — people were still talking about it. He nodded. He looked both ways and then leaned in. "Deek got a B-plus the other day," he whispered. "He couldn't even believe it. That's the kind of grade that's gonna keep him on the team."

"You tell him I better see him at the library on Saturday," I whispered. "Just to make sure!"

"You're all right, Amar'e," said Isaac.

Coach B gave us a quick speech to fire us up, but it wasn't even necessary. We flew out of the locker room and into the gym. Once we burst in, the bleachers roared. I looked around: This place was packed to the rafters!

The teams took the court for the opening tip. Ten kids, and I wasn't one of them. I took my spot on the bench next to Gerry and we kept ourselves busy cheering on our team. I even managed a few hoots when Kurt scored on a put-back.

I would've cheered for him again — if he'd scored again. But apart from that short put-back, he was ice-cold from the field. The Cougar defense had something to do with it. They had a tall guy with really long arms. He was stuck to Kurt like paint on a wall. That let them double-team Bibo every time he got the ball.

Meanwhile, their center was big, and their point guard was quick. Everywhere on the court, points were hard to come by. I could see why they won the title last year. They didn't seem to have any weaknesses. Coach knew it, too.

"Defense!" he called. "Buckle down!"

If we weren't lighting it up, we had to make sure they weren't, either. Our starters did a good enough job of it that the Cougars called a time-out to talk things over five minutes in.

"Get in here! Get in here!" Coach B called.

"All right, we're going to mix things up a little," said Coach as the time-out wound down. "Isaac, you switch over to shooting guard. Bibo, you bring the ball up. Kurt, you take a breather."

Kurt nodded. He wasn't surprised: He'd been a brick factory out there. The only question now was who'd come in to replace him. Coach looked right at me. "Amar'e," he said.

I stood up. "Yeah, Coach?"

"You've got some length. See what you can do against that big ol' beanpole!"

I took my own quick look up into the stands: Mike, Deuce, Dougie, and the rest of my friends had a row to themselves. Junior had camped his big frame along the aisle, like a bouncer. I took a deep breath and headed for the court. I heard Jammer's voice in my head: "Get out there and operate."

I intended to. Of course, my defender had other ideas. Up close, he looked less like a beanpole and more like a gigantic praying mantis. Before the whistle even blew, I could tell this guy was really going to bug me.

CHAPTER 17

Having Bibo handling the ball created all kinds of confusion for the other team. They still double-teamed him, but it's pretty risky to double a guy who's looking to pass. I was happy to help demonstrate why. Bibo dribbled past and my guy drifted over to try to cut him off in the corner. That left me free to slip down the baseline.

I looked back, hoping Bibo would notice. He was penned in. My guy had his long arms straight up in the air, blocking off the pass over the top. Meanwhile, his guy was swatting and grabbing at the ball. For a second, I thought Bibo might've made a mistake and gotten himself trapped there. Then I saw him duck to the side.

We made eye contact, but his expression told me more than his eyes. He was smiling!

Quick as a cobra, he whipped the ball around the side of the praying mantis in front of him. The ball was actually out of bounds for most of its flight, but it was just inside the line when it hit. It bounced right up into my hands. I turned and saw clear sailing to the hoop. The nearest defender was on the other side of the rim. There was nothing he could do as I finger-rolled it up and in.

"Stay with the new guy, Fabrice!" the Cougars coach shouted from the bench. "New guy's a scorer!"

I liked the sound of that. I also liked knowing my defender's name. No offense to anyone named Fabrice, but it's a lot less intimidating than thinking of him as a giant bug.

A few plays later, Bibo and I did the same thing. We weren't on the baseline this time. We were at the high post at the top of the free throw line, but the players were the same. Sure enough, Fabrice did what his coach had told him. He stayed with me as I drifted toward the hoop.

And that opened up aaaaaall that space. As soon as we got deep enough, I shot around and got in front of him. I held my postion as Bibo came flying straight at us. His defender was scrambling to catch up and mine was pinned behind me. Bibo stopped and popped: two more for the Bears. We fist-bumped and headed back up the court.

Fabrice was making me work hard on defense. I did my best to stay tall and deny him the ball. The game had loosened up now. We'd gotten them out of position on defense but, well, that had kind of gotten us out of position, too. Isaac was at shooting guard. He could shoot well enough, but he was a little small to guard the Cougar shooting guard, a sharpshooter named Muni. I was too far away to do anything about it as Muni slipped past Isaac, grabbed his own rebound, and flipped it up and in.

That tied the score at 22–all.

The next time down, I decided to go right at Fabrice. I knew from the tournaments that sometimes these big guys weren't used to that. Fabrice reminded me a lot of that guy Oakley in my last tourney. There was some rapid-fire passing around the perimeter: Bibo to Deek to Isaac, who saw me down low and fired a chest pass to me. I turned right away and went up with the ball. Fabrice left his feet. Psych! I pulled the ball back and ducked underneath him to complete the up-and-under move.

His space-bug arms were so long that he was still able to reach behind and swat at the shot. He slapped me hard across the arm. The shot went wide, but the whistle blew.

"Relaxed and smooth," I told myself at the line. In his spot on the edge of the lane, I saw Kelvin nod. A drop of sweat fell from his chin. He'd been a beast on the boards all game. I hit the first. Everyone tensed for the rebound before the second, but the ball went right through.

The whistle blew for subs. I looked over to see who was coming in for me. The answer: no one.

"You got the hot hand, Amar'e," said Bibo. "Let's keep it going." Kidding! He didn't say anything — this was still Bibo we were talking about. He just gave me a nod as we waited for the new guys to take their positions.

The game stayed tight, and I did my part with two more buckets. Then a few bad bounces and missed shots right at the end of the half sent us into the locker room down 32–28. I thought Coach B would be mad, but Deek leaned in and gave me the scoop. "This is a lot closer than the last time we played them."

We were knee-deep in X's and O's after that. "We're gonna go back to our regular positions to start the second," said Coach toward the end. "They're not doubling Mark as much, and we need to clamp down a little better on defense."

For a few moments, it seemed like that was all he was going to say. But then he looked around the room and added: "I think the team is starting to come together. We're getting contributions from our leaders — and our new guys. We're getting something from everyone, and that's a team."

He didn't mention me by name, but he didn't need to. It was a genius halftime speech, because when you mention everyone, everyone gets fired up! We came out of that locker room like we'd been fired from a cannon. We went from down four to tied in a minute and change.

Their coach called a time-out after that. He must have worked some magic of his own, because things stiffened up after that. Kurt came back in for me. But a few bricks later, he was right back out. As much of a jerk as he'd been to me, I still felt bad for him. Biggest game of the season, and he was ice-cold.

I shook it off. I had bigger things to worry about — namely Fabrice's arms! We both knew we were in a battle now, and we had the sweat-soaked jerseys to prove it. He scored over me with a few hook shots. I scored with a fadeaway jumper and got him again with the up-and-under. Two points for the hoop, and one for the foul.

The lead went back and forth and the game went down to the wire. Muni had gotten hot from the outside. He was the guy who'd given Isaac fits. Now he was causing Bibo trouble with his range. On the other end, they were back to doubling Bibo on almost every possession. Even worse: They'd gotten better at it.

With two minutes to go, Muni hit a long jumper to put them up by two. With just under a minute to go, Bibo saw enough daylight in the double team to dump the ball down to Kelvin. He got hacked on the way up and went to the line.

Now I was the one on the edge of the lane. The home crowd was quiet as he prepared for the free throws. "Relaxed and smooth," I said, and he nodded. He made the first shot to cut the Cougars' lead to one. There was a quick substitution: Gerry came in for Isaac. Then everyone in the building held their breath as the second shot went up.

It looked smooth. It looked relaxed. It rimmed out.

"We need a stop!" bellowed Coach B.

This was crunch time, and I'll be honest: I was dog tired. I'd gone from a couple of minutes a game to nearly the whole thing. I needed energy, and I was pretty sure I knew where I could get it. As we sprinted back up the court, I took a quick look up in the bleachers.

Junior's spot at the end of the row was taken by an even larger figure: Dad! He'd come straight from work. The sleeves of his work shirt were rolled up, and Junior was leaning in and saying something to him. Probably catching him up on what he'd missed. Next to them,

Mike, Deuce, and Dougie saw me looking up. They pointed down and cheered me on.

I could feel my batteries charging. This was my team down here, but that was my team up there, too. I was playing for both of them.

We pressured the ball, but they got it inside to Fabrice. Seconds were ticking away. If he scored here, we were toast. I was right up on him, and he started going into a series of moves that had become way too familiar. "Hook, hook, hook!" I shouted.

I could pressure him, but with those arms of his, there was no way I could block his hook shot. I had to rely on my teammates. Fortunately, I had some good ones. Gerry — the guy who'd listened to me before anyone else on the team — heard me again. He swung his head around just as Fabrice was bringing the ball back. He reached out with those fast, point-guard hands and swatted it.

Suddenly, the ball was loose in the lane. More precious seconds ticked off the clock as everyone scrambled for it. It was Kelvin who got his big mitts on it. He got it to Gerry, and we all raced up court. As soon as we got the ball onto our half of the court, Coach called our last time-out.

I looked at the clock: ten seconds.

Remember when I said before that it was crunch time? I take it back. *This* was crunch time. We leaned in as Coach drew up our final play. "It's gotta go to Bibo," said Isaac, who was coming back in for the final possession.

Bibo nodded. He was a baller and wouldn't back down from taking the big shot. But Coach wasn't sure. "They'll expect that," he said. "And that double team has been tough."

He looked around at us. Finally, his eyes stopped on me. "Think you can get another one past him?"

I nodded. There was one thing I hadn't tried yet.

Coach made up his mind. "If Mark's doubled, look for Amar'e," he said.

We headed back out for the play that could make or break our season. I felt good. All the gaps were gone. My friends were here to support me. And that other thing that was missing, the thing I couldn't quite put my finger on: I knew what it was now. It was contributing, being right in the thick of the action.

Now I just had to finish strong and make sure this feeling didn't turn to mud. Kelvin inbounded to Isaac. The double team clamped down on Bibo like two sides of a vise. Now I knew the ball was coming my way. I cut toward the hoop, and Isaac found me.

Fabrice was in front of me, his long arms spread out like sails. He had good position. Normally, I would have passed the ball back out. But there was nothing normal about this. We had four seconds left and needed to score. I had time for one move.

I dribbled right at him. His big frame engulfed me like a shadow. And then I spun. For a second, I didn't even know where he was. I was concentrating on my feet. So many bad things could happen. I could almost hear the sound of the ref's whistle or the slap of Fabrice's hand on the ball as my shot went up.

Almost.

But the whistle didn't blow. The play was clean. And those big hands came up empty. As soon as the ball left my hand, the clock wasn't an issue. I watched its flight.

Fabrice turned and watched it, too. It hit the backboard and dropped down onto the rim. The muscles in our legs went slack as the horn sounded. There would be no rebound.

The ball teetered there. My eyes were wide open as I watched. I was afraid to blink, but it turned out I didn't need my eyes at all. The roar of the home crowd told me everything I needed to know.

Things were pretty crazy after the win. But one thing didn't change: The first thing I did was congratulate my teammates. It was easier this time, since a lot of them were coming up to me. "Nice shot!" I heard as I headed toward the sideline. "Great game!"

I high-fived Gerry, Isaac, and Kelvin right in a row. They'd all played hard and had good games, and I told them so. Then I saw Bibo and no words were necessary. We bumped fists and nodded, as usual. It was a tradition I was really starting to like.

Kurt was right behind him, talking to Deek and Joe again. I remembered how he'd left me hanging before. That's why I was surprised when he extended his fist first. For a second, I thought about leaving *him* hanging. But just for a second. He was still my teammate.

"Good game," I said as we bumped fists.

"Nah, I stunk it up out there, man," he said. "I stunk it up, and you bailed us out. I'll be back next game, but it's good to know you're here."

Deek picked up the thought. "We're all in eighth," he said. "This is our last year. But with you and Bibo, your friend Gerry over there, the Bears'll be in good hands."

Kurt nodded, but then a sly smile crept across his face. "Of course, we've got some serious work to do until then, just to make sure you're fully prepared."

Now I smiled. "I have no doubt about that."

"Anyway," said Joe as we all started to move on, "good game today. Welcome to the Bears."

And coming from the "permanent ref," I think that was official.

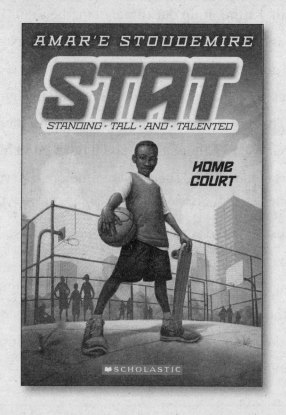

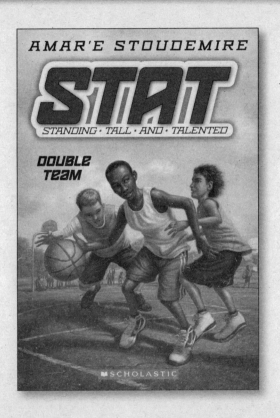

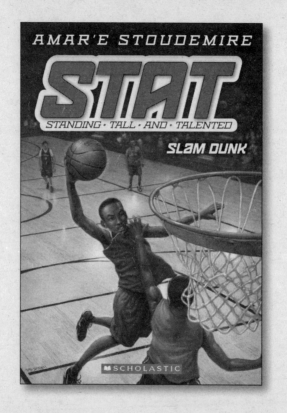